We Love Holidays
PASSOVER

Saviour Pirotta

PowerKiDS
press.

New York

Saviour Pirotta is a highly experienced author, who has written many books for young children. He was born in Malta and is also a trained chef.

Published in 2008 by The Rosen Publishing Group, Inc.
29 East 21st Street, New York, NY 10010

First Edition

The publishers would like to thank the following for allowing us to reproduce their pictures in this book:

Wayland Picture Library: 6, 12, 20 / Sonia Halliday: 5, 6, 7, 11 / Corbis: title page 21, Roger Ressmeyer; 23, Philip de Bay / Alamy: 16, Steve Allan, 10, Eitan Simanor, 22, World Religions Photo Library; 15, Network Photographers, 18, Photofusion Picture Library / Getty Images: 4, Baerbel Schmidt; 17, Formula Z/S; 9, Ancient Art and Architecture / Art Directors: 13, Juliette Soester, 14, Itzhak Genut, 19, Helene Rogers.

Library of Congress Cataloging-in-Publication Data
Pirotta, Saviour.
    Passover / Saviour Pirotta. -- 1st ed.
        p. cm. -- (We love holidays)
    Includes index.
    ISBN-13: 978-1-4042-3707-0 (library binding)
    ISBN-10: 1-4042-3707-0 (library binding)

    1. Passover--Juvenile literature. 2. Seder--Juvenile literature.
I. Title.
BM695.P3P52 2007
296.4'37--dc22

7769   2006026790

Manufactured in China

Contents

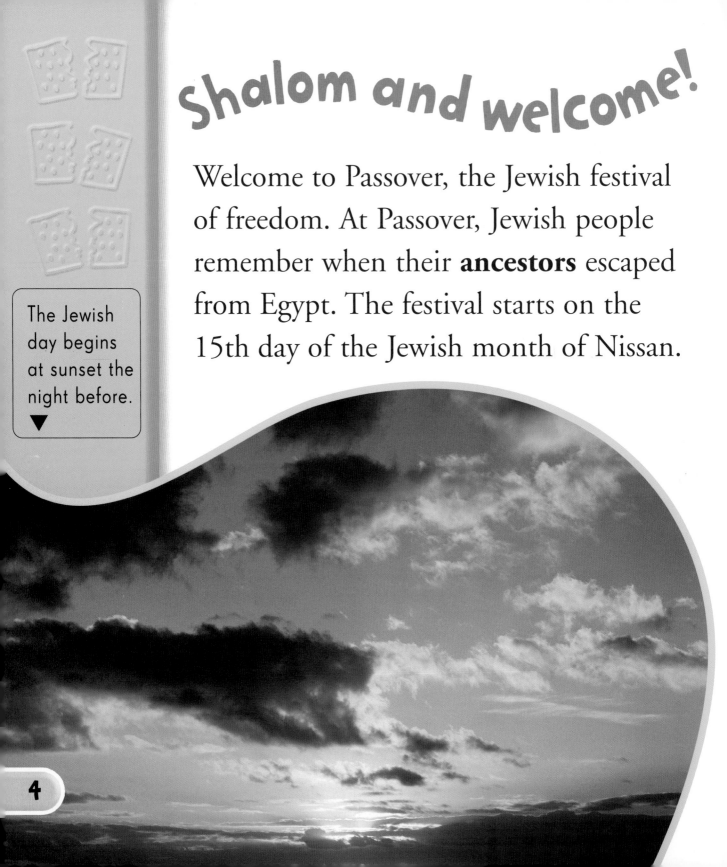

Shalom and welcome!

Welcome to Passover, the Jewish festival of freedom. At Passover, Jewish people remember when their **ancestors** escaped from Egypt. The festival starts on the 15th day of the Jewish month of Nissan.

The Jewish day begins at sunset the night before. ▼

Look, the sun is setting.
A new day is beginning.
It is time
to start.

Jewish children play an important part in Passover. ◀

5

Let my people go!

A long time ago, the Jewish people had no freedom. They were slaves in Egypt. But God wanted them to be free.

A plague of locusts ate all the grain in Egypt.

He ordered a Jewish shepherd called Moses to demand their freedom, but the Egyptian **Pharaoh** would not let them go. God sent ten **plagues** to punish the Egyptians.

passed over

It took one last punishment, the tenth plague, to convince the Pharaoh to free the Jewish slaves. The eldest boy in each Egyptian house was to die.

A mysterious disease killed all the Pharaoh's farm animals. ▶

But God told the Jewish people to mark the doors of their houses with lamb's blood. That way Death "passed over" their houses, and the Jewish children were saved.

Freedom at last

This baker is making dough to roll into **matzos** for Passover. ▶

When the Egyptians lost their eldest sons, the Pharaoh set the Jewish people free. The slaves left in such a hurry, there was no time to make bread for the journey. In the desert, they baked flat loaves called **matzos**.

DID YOU KNOW?

Some Egyptians paid the
Jewish people with gold and
silver to leave Egypt.

Since then,
the flat loaves
have become
the symbol
of Passover.

◄
Matzos, like
the ones these
children are
eating, are
flat because
they have no
yeast in
them.

11

cleaning out the house

Matzos and special Passover food can be found in stores before the festival.
▼

No food with yeast in it is eaten during Passover. Before the festival starts, Jewish people get rid of every scrap of bread, cakes, and cookies.

They even clean
their offices and stores.
Eating only food without
yeast reminds them of
the Jews fleeing Egypt.

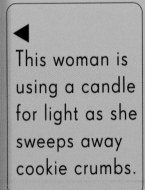

◀ This woman is
using a candle
for light as she
sweeps away
cookie crumbs.

13

No more yeast

The day before Passover, Jewish families do a final search in the house for food with yeast in it. If they find any, they put it in a bag and burn it.

14

DID YOU KNOW?

First-born sons go without food the day before Passover, to thank God for saving the Jewish boys in Egypt.

Now the house is clean or "**kosher**." The festival can begin.

These people have come together to burn their food with yeast in it. ◄

15

Seder food

On each of the first two nights of Passover, Jewish people eat a meal called a **Seder**.

The foods of Seder are eaten in a special order. ▶

16

On the table is a Seder plate with different foods on it. Each item of food reminds people of something about the Jews' escape from slavery in Egypt.

DID YOU KNOW?

A paste of apple and walnuts is a reminder of the cement the Jewish slaves used for building.

Retelling the story

During the Seder meal, the grown-ups read out loud from the **Haggadah**, the book that tells how the Jews escaped from Egypt. The book also has songs, prayers, and blessings.

These people are dipping their fingers in red wine and spilling a drop on their plates in memory of the plagues.
▶

DID YOU KNOW?

The youngest child at the table asks his or her father four questions about Seder night.

This illustration is from the Haggadah. It shows the ten plagues that God sent to punish the Egyptians.

▼

A drop of wine is spilled for each of the ten plagues. This shows how sad people are that their freedom caused the Egyptians a lot of pain and suffering.

Find the Matzo

During the meal, three matzos are used. A piece of the second one is hidden around the house by the parents. At the end of the meal the child who finds it gets a prize!

Children look forward to finding the hidden matzo. They share it with their family. ▶

DID YOU KNOW?

Grown-ups drink four cups of wine during the Seder meal to remind them of God's promises.

This family has a special silver tray on which the three matzos are placed. ▼

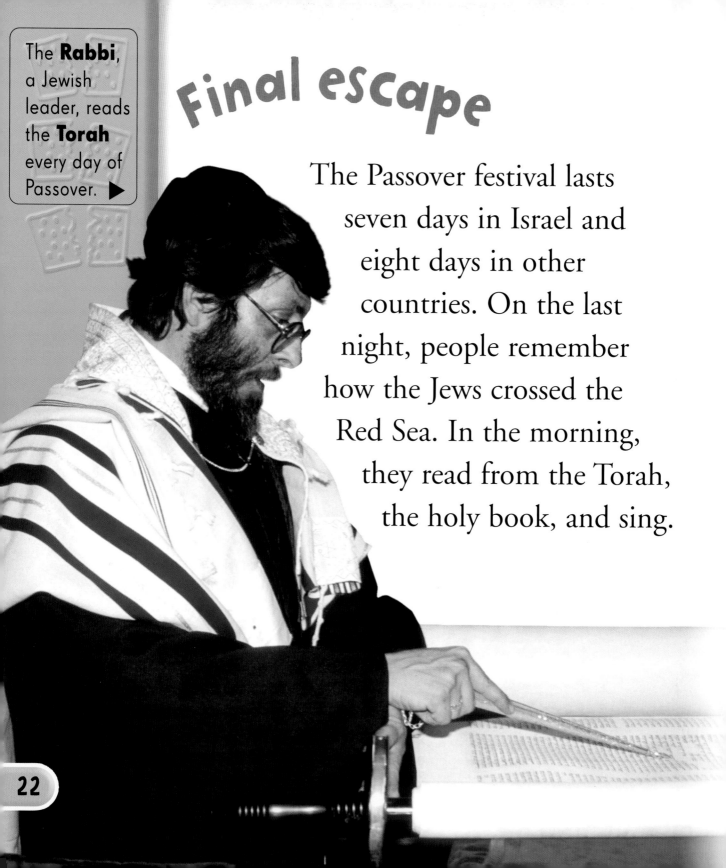

The **Rabbi**, a Jewish leader, reads the **Torah** every day of Passover. ▶

Final escape

The Passover festival lasts seven days in Israel and eight days in other countries. On the last night, people remember how the Jews crossed the Red Sea. In the morning, they read from the Torah, the holy book, and sing.

◄
This picture shows Moses parting the Red Sea so that the Jews could escape from Egypt.

Then it's time to put away the special pots and pans. Another Passover festival is over.

Index

Glossary

ancestors people that we are related to, from a long time ago

Haggadah the book used for telling the story of Passover

Hebrew the ancient Jewish language

kosher food that is prepared following Jewish law

matzo/matzos (plural) flat bread that is made without using yeast

Pharaoh an ancient Egyptian ruler

plague a pest or disease that spreads quickly over a wide area

pyramids ancient Egyptian tombs with sloping sides

Rabbi a Jewish leader

Seder the Jewish service and dinner at Passover

Torah the Jewish holy scrolls

yeast an ingredient used to make bread rise

JAN   2010